S0-BXM-471

Thank you for your support!

THE Scolbrine

Sheila Chartrand

Illustrated by Kallie Chartrand

MERRY 2022 Christmas Myla
Love gr Ray
& gr Kelly

Library and Archives Canada Cataloguing in Publication

Chartrand, Sheila, 1969-, author
    The schobrine / written by Sheila Chartrand ; illustrated by Kallie Chartrand.

(Come over to my house ; 1)
ISBN 978-0-9919335-1-8 (bound)

    I. Chartrand, Kallie, illustrator II. Title. III. Series: Come over to my house ; 1

PS8605.H3844S36 2013   jC813'.6   C2013-907785-5

Cover design by Kallie Chartrand
Cover layout by UNÉ Productions
Special thank you to Dustin Tilley-Sturgeon, Vivid Designs Ltd.

Printed in Canada

April Dew Publishing
1 - 504 Delmar Avenue
Pointe Claire, QC
Canada H9R 4A6
www.aprildew.com

In Loving Memory of My Son

Corey Réal Joseph Chartrand

"Big C"

January 6, 1994 – December 20, 2010

My Gentle Giant with a Heart of Gold
You will forever be loved and missed… ♥

**A DONATION WILL BE MADE TO THE KIDS FOREVER
CHARITY FROM THE SALE OF EACH BOOK.**

Kids Forever is a non-profit organization, founded in 1997 in Fort McMurray, Alberta by John Foy in the basement of his home. John made it his mission to help families with sick children and special needs. Every cent of the monies collected and donated through this Charity goes directly to assist the families with medical and travel expenses, specialized equipment and aid in coping with their illness and disabilities. To date, they have helped hundreds of families.

Kids Forever also strongly believes in keeping alive the memory of children who have passed away, hence, the aptly named program, "Keeping Their Memories Alive". The program donates large amounts to hospitals, care facilities and youth camps in the memory of the child and a commemorative plaque that is displayed in the facility.

As quoted at the 16th Annual Kids Forever Fundraising event:
"The world is a better place today because you have made a difference in the life of a child" - John Foy

www.kidsforever.ca

The Schobrine

sh–chō ' / brīne

A "Come Over To My House" Series

Book 1

Based on a true story

Come over to my house, come over to play,

So that I can tell you what happened today.

My brother and I, we wanted a pet,

We wanted a pet more that anything yet!

We begged and we pleaded, "Please listen to us,

Our pet will be good; it won't make a big fuss."

Our parents then said, "I do not really know.

Pets need good care to be healthy and grow.

Maybe you should both wait 'til you're older,

Winter is coming and the nights will get colder."

We want a nice pet to live in our house.

"You both can forget about wanting a mouse!

Your Daddy can't stand them, he doesn't like mice,

Your pet must be one that we all think is nice!"

"What kind of pet are you thinking of now?

You both can forget about wanting a cow!"

"Cows live on farms, not in cities you see."

My Father then said, as he looked right at me.

"I watched a show that was on yesterday,"

"What about something that likes to eat hay?"

"A camel, a horse or a lamb we can keep!

How about getting a whole herd of sheep?"

Our parents both looked at us and then they said,

"We don't have enough hay to keep them all fed."

My brother and I then said with a smile,

"What about getting a green crocodile?"

"I really don't think so," our Father had said,

"He'd nibble your toes while you sleep in your bed!"

"Keep thinking," they said, "Keep thinking you two.

We don't want to turn our house into a zoo!"

"A pigeon, a duck or a bird that can't fly!

An ostrich can not take off into the sky."

"A bird," said our Mommy, "is not for the best.

It might turn your bedrooms into a big nest."

"Why not get a goldfish?" my Daddy then said.

"No good," said my brother, "I want something red!"

"A lizard, a snake or a tiny small newt?"

"Not really," said Mommy, "they'll hide in your boot!"

"A lion, a tiger or something that's wild?"

"No way!" said my Daddy, "They'll swallow a child!"

"A baboon, a monkey, we have lots of trees!"

"Let's get one!" I said as I begged on my knees.

"No way!" said our Mother, "You'll have to keep thinking."

"Oh Mommy!" I said, "Our ideas keep sinking!"

"I've got it!" said Corey, "We'll get a big bat."

"Never!" said Kallie, "I won't care for that!"

We sat and we thought about what we would get,

"What in the world would we choose for a pet?"

"An elephant, a zebra, or maybe an ox?

We could try taming a little red fox!"

"No good!" said my sister, "Not something so big."

"Why not get a gopher, they just like to dig?"

"No rodents!" said Mommy, "I told you not that!

No leopards, no cougars, no big jungle cats!"

"Hippos or peacocks don't make a good pet!

Have you decided on anything yet?"

"No turtles or frogs because they eat bugs,

No polar bears either, they give big bear hugs!"

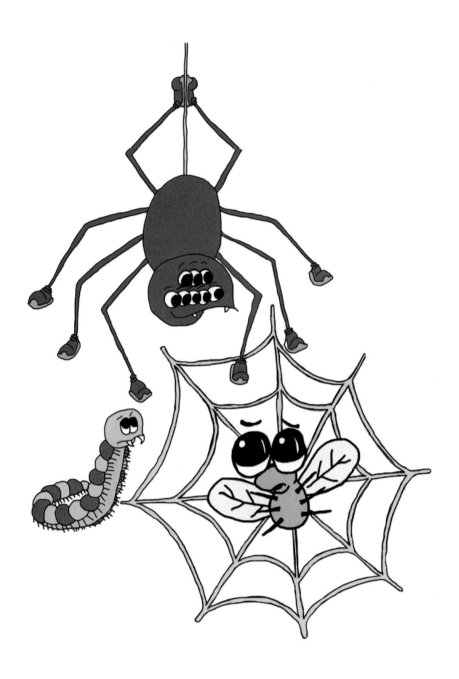

"No insects or spiders, they're creepy and crawly,

I want you to choose one that is really jolly!"

"Remember that all pets need lots of good care,

Cleaning feathers or fur or ones with no hair!"

"With bunnies and rabbits, they eat lots of carrots,

The climate's too cold here for tropical parrots."

"No sharks or big whales or fish from the sea,"

Our Daddy then said, "Will you listen to me?"

Right after he said, "We'll get a Schobrine,

You'll come to love it, just give it some time!"

"The Schobrine can stay in or it can go out,

Just let me finish, do not start to pout!"

"Some feedings with water, you'll give it each day,

A Schobrine will make a good pet that will play!"

"What is a Schobrine?" we both wondered then said,

"Can it come inside, to sleep on my bed?"

"Yes it can," said my Daddy, "It's furry and cute."

"Is it a penguin that's dressed in a suit?"

"A Schobrine has whiskers, four feet and two ears."

"Is it a moose or some cute baby deers?"

"Is it an elk or a big buffalo?

Tell me, please tell me. I really don't know!"

"A Schobrine can be any colour or size."

"Is it an owl that is very wise?"

"Keep guessing," said Daddy, "You're both doing well."

"Is it a chipmunk that makes his cheeks swell?"

"A raccoon, an otter or maybe a goat?

Is it a swimmer that knows how to float?"

"A Schobrine is something that purrs all the time."

"Is it a guard dog that helps to fight crime?"

Daddy then said, "A Schobrine is a cat!"

"Oh Mommy," we both said, "We'd really like that!"

We went to a shelter and adopted a kitten,

She was the size of my fuzzy blue mitten.

"We promise to feed and to love her each day,

Sasha, our cat, has now come here to stay!"

About the Author:

Sheila Chartrand was raised in the small rural community of Grimshaw, Alberta in the Peace Country. Upon graduation, she moved to Fort McMurray, Alberta to attend college where she met her future husband, Réal Chartrand. They had two children, a girl and boy that completed their family. *'The Schobrine'* is based upon one of the many experiences Sheila and Réal shared with their children during their childhood. It is the first book from the *'Come Over To My House'* series. Each book in the series is a precious memory that can only be labelled as priceless.

Sheila comments, "The bond that grows between a mother and her children is nothing short of a miracle," and also states that her life is so much richer because of them. This book is dedicated in loving memory of her son, Corey who was tragically killed in an automobile accident at the tender age of 16. "All I have left of my dear son is the love and the memories, and I will cherish every single one of them. You must keep the memories alive".

Sheila still resides in Fort McMurray with her husband. Together, they own two successful businesses.

About the Illustrator:

Kallie Chartrand, Sheila's daughter was born and raised in Fort McMurray, Alberta where she still lives today. While growing up, imagination was encouraged by her parents in everyday activities, adventures and lessons. Family time was and still is extremely important in daily life.

Kallie's gentle compassion and nature led her to becoming a registered nurse with a Bachelor of Science in Nursing. While working on a surgery and paediatrics unit, she tries to bring a smile into every room she enters. Kallie hopes to use her nursing to help others regain their strength when they are in their greatest moments of weakness.

Kallie notes, "The *'Come Over To My House'* series will touch the lives of so many. Children will spend quality time reading the stories with their loved ones, while donations from the purchase of each book will be used to relieve another family's financial burdens due to their child being sick or having special needs, or due to the need for specialized medical equipment."

She would like to thank each and every person for their purchase and helping to make a difference in another's life.